MURDEROUS MOSQUITOES

by Meish Goldish

Consultant: Eric S. Loker, PhD
Distinguished Professor and Curator
Division of Parasitology
Museum of Southwestern Biology
The University of New Mexico

BEARPORT
PUBLISHING

New York, New York

Credits

Cover, © khlungcenter/Shutterstock; TOC, © Somboon Bunproy/Shutterstock; 4L, © Nataly Reinch/Shutterstock; 4R, © Handout/MCT/Newscom; 5, © Sirirat Savettanant/Dreamstime; 6, © Medicshots/Alamy; 7L, © Antonio Perez/MCT/Newscom; 7R, © Antonio Perez/MCT/Newscom; 8, © tskstock/iStock; 9T, © RAJ CREATIONZS/Shutterstock; 9B, © Rawpixel.com/Shutterstock; 10, © Xinhua/Alamy; 11, © Ueslei Marcelino/Reuters; 12, © F1online digitale Bildagentur GmbH/Alamy; 13T, © Tomasz Resiak/Dreamstime; 13B, © Kerrick/iStock; 14, © Nature Picture Library/Alamy; 15T, © Genevieve Vallee/Alamy; 15B, © Des Willie/Alamy; 16T, © B. Borrell Casals/FLPA/Minden; 16B, © Astrid Gast/Shutterstock; 17T, © doug4537/iStock; 17B, © Nature Picture Library/Alamy; 18, © M & P Fogden/Minden Pictures/AGE Fotostock; 19T, © Marta NavarroP/Shutterstock; 19B, © Zuma Press Inc./Alamy; 20, © dorioconnell/iStock; 21, © Elizaveta/Shutterstock; 22 (T to B), © BSIP SA/Alamy, © RobertoDavid/iStock, and © BSIP SA/Alamy.

Publisher: Kenn Goin
Senior Editor: Joyce Tavolacci
Creative Director: Spencer Brinker
Photo Researcher: Thomas Persano

Library of Congress Cataloging-in-Publication Data

Names: Goldish, Meish, author.
Title: Murderous mosquitoes / by Meish Goldish.
Description: New York, New York : Bearport Publishing, [2019] | Series:
    Bugged out! the world's most dangerous bugs |
    Includes bibliographical references and index.
Identifiers: LCCN 2018047123 (print) | LCCN 2018048349 (ebook) | ISBN
    9781642802351 (ebook) | ISBN 9781642801668 (library)
Subjects: LCSH: Mosquitoes as carriers of disease—Juvenile literature. |
    Mosquitoes—Juvenile literature.
Classification: LCC RA640 (ebook) | LCC RA640 .G65 2019 (print) | DDC
    614.4/323—dc23
LC record available at https://lccn.loc.gov/2018047123

Copyright © 2019 Bearport Publishing Company, Inc. All rights reserved. No part of this publication may be reproduced in whole or in part, stored in any retrieval system, or transmitted in any form or by any means, electronic, mechanical, photocopying, recording, or otherwise, without written permission from the publisher.

For more information, write to Bearport Publishing Company, Inc., 45 West 21st Street, Suite 3B, New York, New York 10010. Printed in the United States of America.

10 9 8 7 6 5 4 3 2 1

Contents

A Dangerous Bite 4
Struggling to Survive 6
Malaria Attack 8
Small Victims 10
Built for Biting 12
Warm, Wet Homes 14
A Mosquito's Life 16
Another Danger 18
Keeping Safe 20

Other Mosquito-Borne Diseases 22
Glossary 23
Index 24
Bibliography 24
Read More 24
Learn More Online 24
About the Author 24

A Dangerous Bite

In February 2008, Dawn Dubsky of Chicago spent a two-week vacation in Ghana, a country in West Africa. One day while Dawn sat by a swimming pool, she heard a mosquito buzzing nearby. Before she knew it, the tiny insect landed on her right leg and bit her. Dawn quickly forgot about the small bite.

A resort in Ghana like the one where Dawn Dubsky was bitten by a mosquito

Dawn, who's a nurse, on vacation in Ghana

Upon returning to Chicago, Dawn felt weak and had a throbbing headache. One night, she woke up with a high fever and her body was soaked in sweat. Dawn decided to check herself into the hospital. A blood test revealed she had a life-threatening disease called **malaria**. However, Dawn's doctors weren't worried. It seemed like a mild case that could easily be cured with medicine. What happened next shocked Dawn and her family.

Some mosquitoes carry tiny **parasites** that cause malaria.

Mosquitoes are tiny flying insects about 0.5 inches (13 mm) long. That's about as wide as a fingernail.

Struggling to Survive

In the hospital, Dawn became sicker as the malaria parasites attacked her body. Her skin turned yellow. Her hands and feet felt so heavy she could barely move. Staring in a mirror, Dawn cried to her mother, "Look at me!" As her lungs and other **organs** began to fail, Dawn's lips turned blue. To help keep her alive, doctors attached Dawn to machines that helped her breathe and operated her **kidneys**.

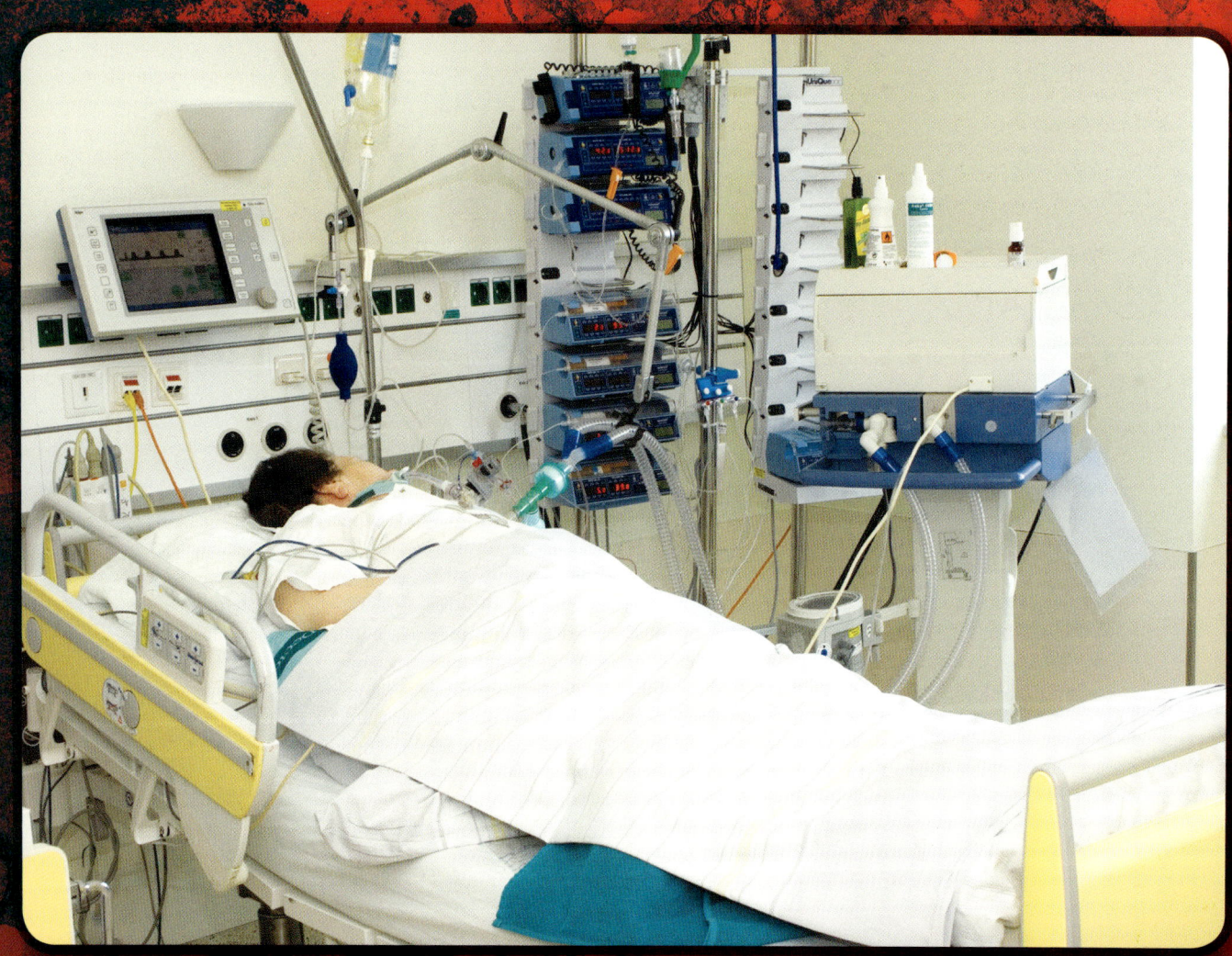

Dawn was connected to special machines, similar to the ones seen here, to keep her alive.

Then the unthinkable happened. When the **tissue** in Dawn's lower arms and legs died due to poor blood flow, doctors had to make a **drastic** decision. They cut off Dawn's arms and legs. Her family was horrified—but the operation saved Dawn's life. Slowly, Dawn got better. She learned to use **prosthetic** arms and legs, which allowed her to lead an active life once again. "That's who Dawn is," her mother said proudly. "She's a fighter."

Dawn practices walking on her new legs.

After recovering, Dawn started an organization called America Against Malaria. It teaches people in Ghana about malaria, and trains doctors and nurses there how to treat it.

Malaria Attack

How can a tiny mosquito make a person so sick? Mosquitoes feed on blood and can spread some of the world's deadliest diseases. For example, when a mosquito bites a person who has malaria, it **ingests** malaria parasites that live in the diseased person's blood. Later, when the mosquito bites a healthy person, the parasites travel from the insect's **saliva** into the victim's body.

This mosquito has just sucked the blood of a human. The blood can be seen in the insect's stomach.

Once inside the victim's body, the malaria parasites quickly multiply. They enter red blood cells and cause them to explode. About a week later, the bite victim may start experiencing **symptoms**, such as headaches, fever, and chills. By then, there are millions of malaria parasites attacking different parts of the body. Without treatment, a person's organs can fail, resulting in death.

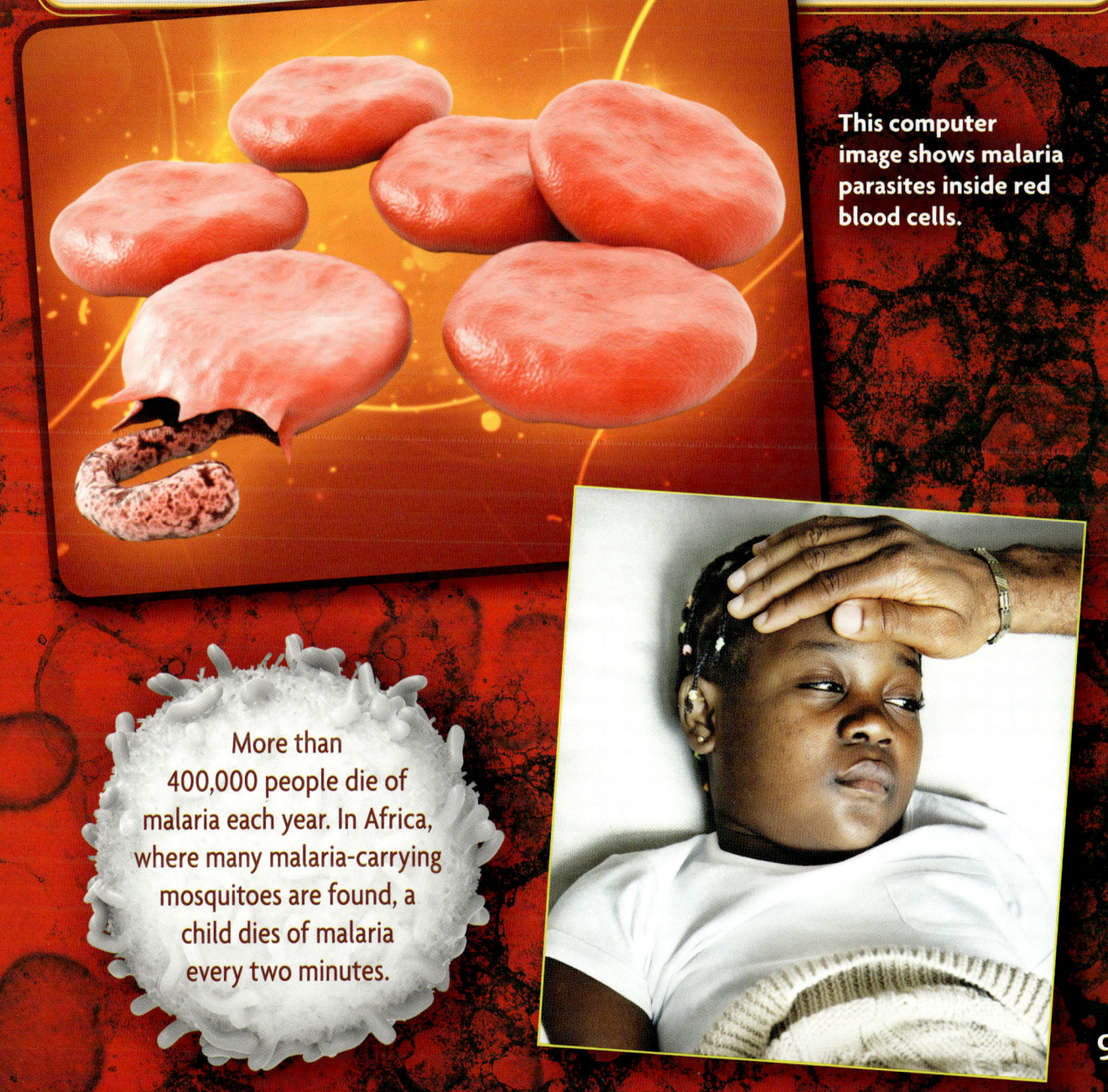

This computer image shows malaria parasites inside red blood cells.

More than 400,000 people die of malaria each year. In Africa, where many malaria-carrying mosquitoes are found, a child dies of malaria every two minutes.

Small Victims

Malaria is not the only dangerous disease that mosquitoes **transmit**. In 2015 in Brazil, a baby named Luiz Felipe was born with a tiny head and brain. His birth **defect** was caused by Zika **virus**. When Luiz's mother was pregnant with him, a mosquito **infected** with Zika bit her. The virus then traveled through her blood to her unborn baby, affecting the growth of his head and brain.

A mother in Brazil holds her baby, who was born with a brain defect caused by Zika virus. Such babies can grow up unable to walk, see, or hear.

Sadly, Luiz is not the only Zika victim. In Brazil alone, thousands of babies have been born with brain defects caused by Zika. Brazilian mothers have formed a support group called United Mothers of Angels. They share their stories to help each other cope. "What gives me strength," Luiz's mother says, "is the love I feel for him and knowing that he's not alone."

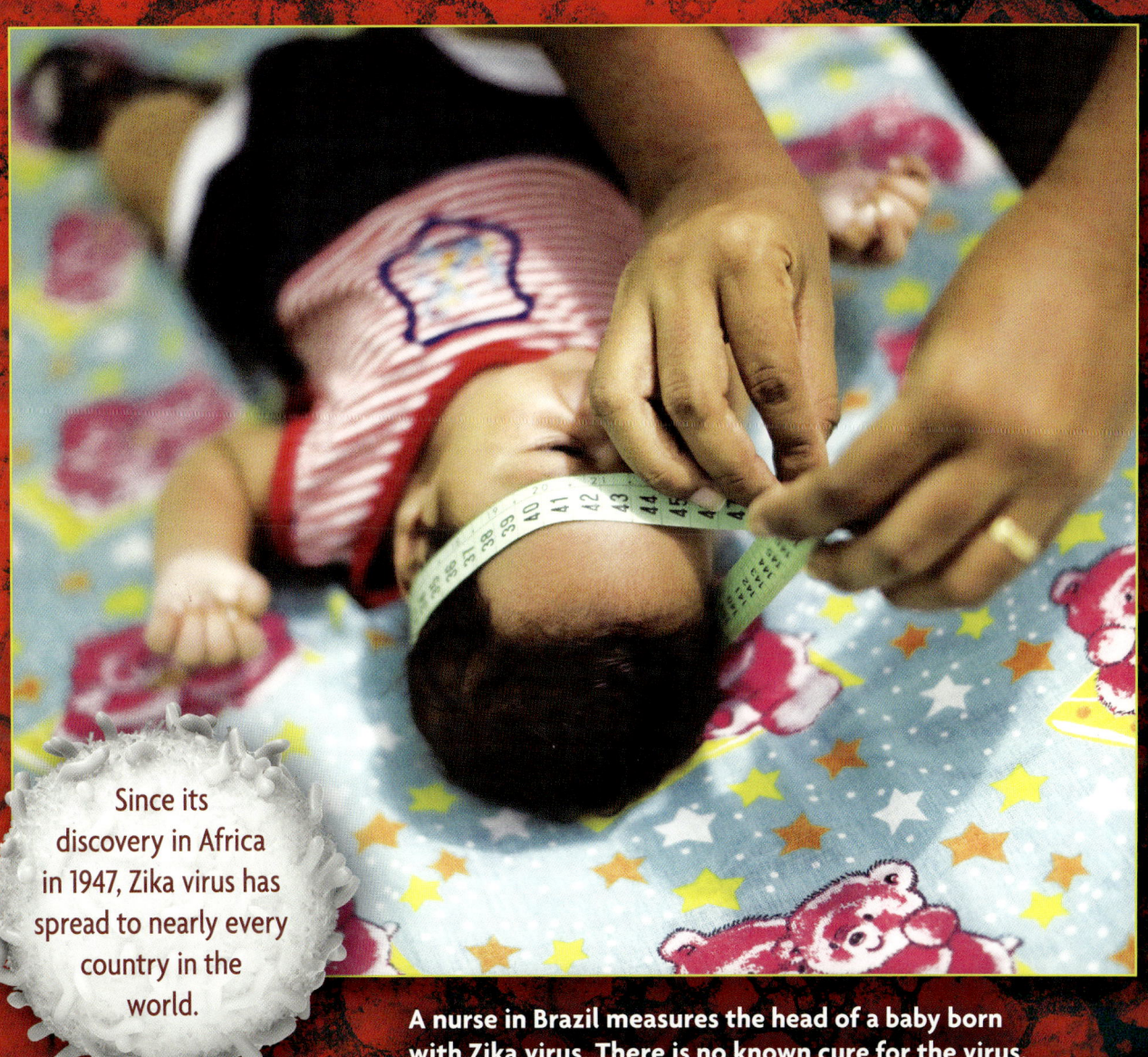

Since its discovery in Africa in 1947, Zika virus has spread to nearly every country in the world.

A nurse in Brazil measures the head of a baby born with Zika virus. There is no known cure for the virus.

11

Built for Biting

A female mosquito is specially built to find a blood meal. It's a tiny but speedy flier able to move a hundred times faster than a human. The insect's two long **antennae** can sense gases in our breath from as far as 200 feet (61 m) away. A mosquito also has two large eyes. They can't focus like a human's eyes, but they can sense quick movements, helping the bloodsucker to zero in on an animal.

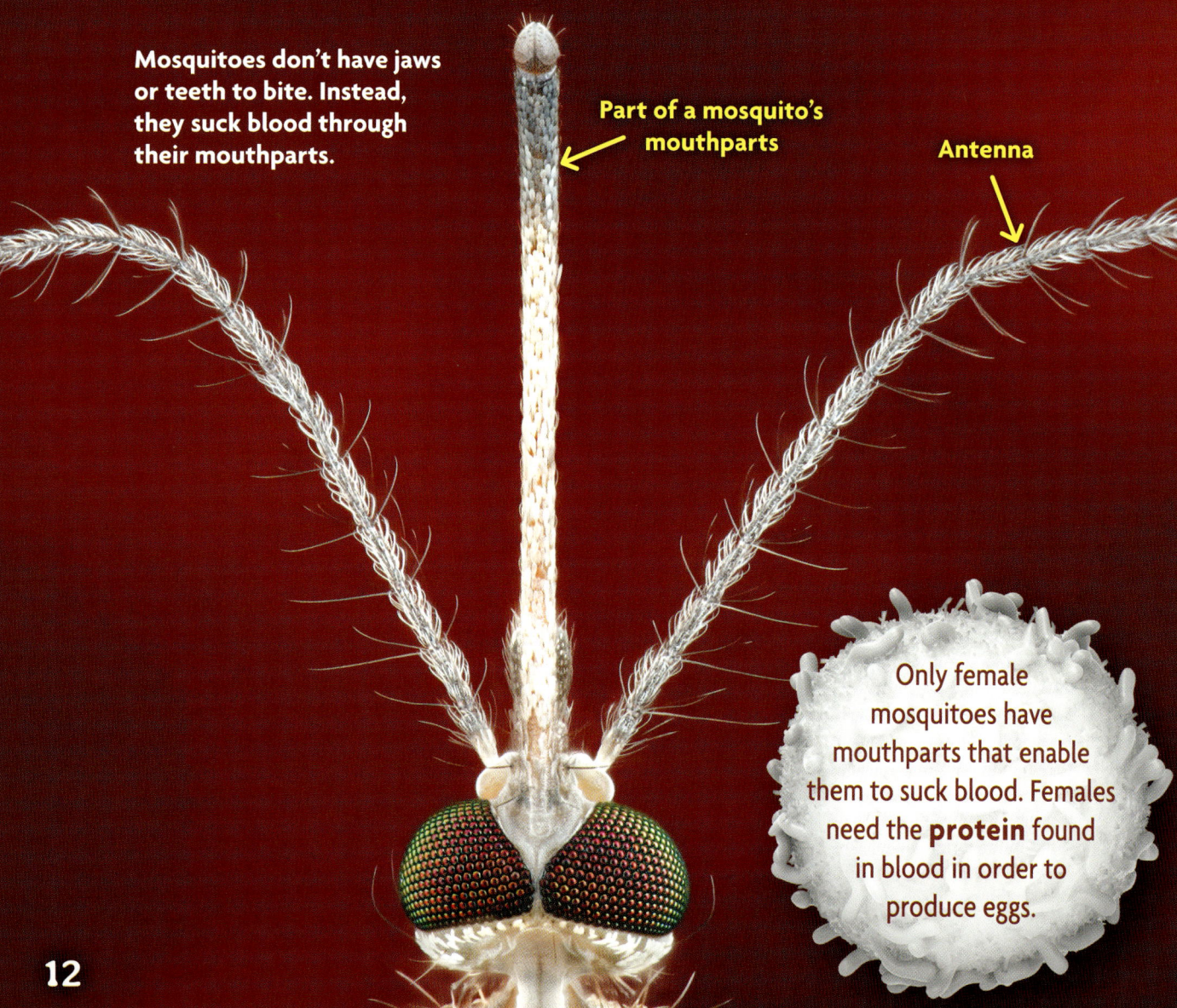

Mosquitoes don't have jaws or teeth to bite. Instead, they suck blood through their mouthparts.

Part of a mosquito's mouthparts

Antenna

Only female mosquitoes have mouthparts that enable them to suck blood. Females need the **protein** found in blood in order to produce eggs.

A mosquito is so light that a person often doesn't feel the insect land on his or her skin. Once in position, the mosquito jabs its **proboscis** into its victim. The proboscis is made up of six tiny needlelike parts called stylets. As the insect sucks its victim's blood through the stylets, it releases saliva to keep the blood from **clotting**. A mosquito can drink up to three times its weight in blood in one feeding. Once its stomach is full, the mosquito flies away.

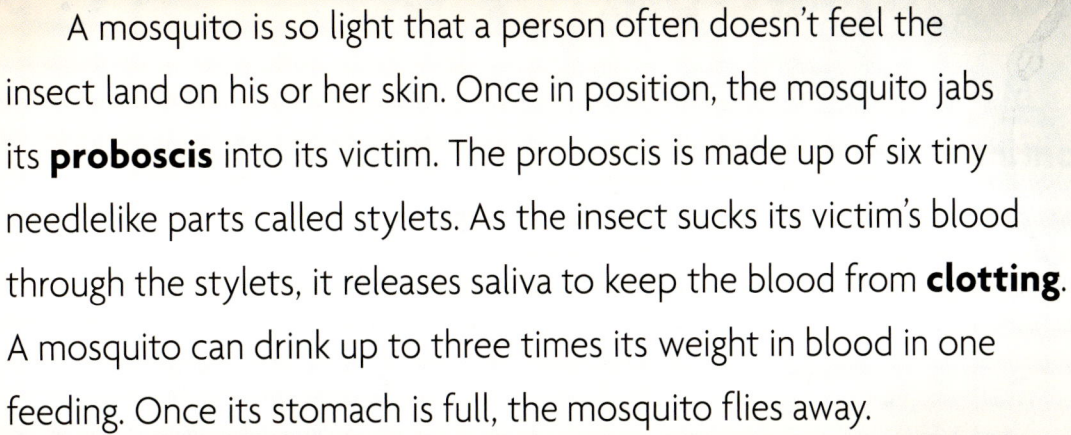

A mosquito's wings can beat 1,000 times per second, creating the familiar whiny, buzzing sound.

Both male and female mosquitoes feed on plant juice called nectar.

A Mosquito's Life

A female may lay up to 300 eggs at a time. After a few days, a **larva** hatches from each egg. The larva looks like a tiny wriggling worm. It feeds on small plants and animals in the water. The larva grows and sheds its skin four times.

Mosquito eggs on a pond

A large group of mosquito eggs is called a raft.

A mosquito laying eggs in water

After about 12 days, a hard, outer covering forms on the larva's body. The insect is now a **pupa**. It rests on the water for one to four days. Then its hard outer covering cracks open, and an adult mosquito with wings crawls out. An adult male lives only a few days. An adult female may live anywhere from a few days to a few months.

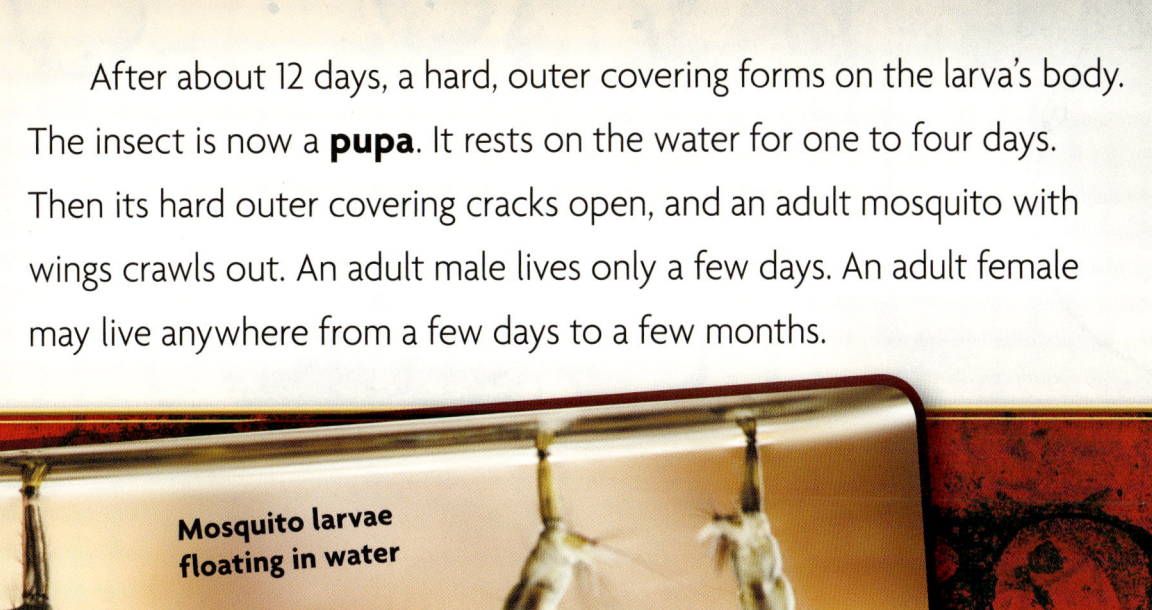

Mosquito larvae floating in water

As an adult, a mosquito can no longer swim and has wings.

Another Danger

Some adult mosquitoes carry a deadly disease called West Nile virus. A mosquito gets the virus by biting an infected bird. Then it passes on the disease to humans through a bite. Many people with West Nile virus have no symptoms. Some victims experience headaches, vomiting, and diarrhea. The worst cases can lead to death.

Mosquitoes feeding on a bird

Mosquitoes can also give West Nile virus to animals, including dogs, cats, horses—and even alligators. In Arizona, a horse named Alex got West Nile virus. As a result, he developed a deadly brain condition called **encephalitis**. Luckily, he survived, but not without brain damage. A trainer spent 18 months caring for Alex and teaching him how to carry a rider again. Thanks to her, Alex was able to lead a mostly normal life.

This horse got encephalitis after being bitten by a mosquito that carried West Nile virus.

About 50 people in North Carolina have died from West Nile virus since 2003. "These infections are rare," warns North Carolina doctor Carl Williams, "but this is a tragic reminder that they can be deadly."

Since 1999, more than 25,000 horses in the United States have been infected with West Nile virus. There is medicine available to prevent horses from getting the disease.

Keeping Safe

Not all mosquitoes carry deadly diseases. In fact, most are harmless—except for the itchy red marks they leave on people's skin. However, the number of people sickened by mosquito-**borne** diseases is going up. According to scientists, one reason is the rise in temperatures around the world. Why? Warmer weather creates more homes for mosquitoes.

A young girl scratches mosquito bites.

What can people do to protect themselves from mosquitoes? The Centers for Disease Control and Prevention (CDC) advises people to use insect **repellent** outdoors and to wear long sleeves and pants. People who get bitten should wash the bite with soap and water. If they feel ill, they should see a doctor immediately. Brazilian doctor Angela Rocha warns, "The whole world needs to be on high alert now."

A person sprays repellent to keep mosquitoes away. Mosquitoes see dark colors better than light colors, so a person wearing light-colored clothing is less likely to get bitten.

Of all the different types of mosquitoes, three kinds are the most dangerous disease carriers. *Anopheles* mosquitoes spread malaria. *Aedes* mosquitoes carry Zika virus. *Culex* mosquitoes transmit West Nile virus.

Other Mosquito-Borne Diseases

In addition to malaria, Zika virus, and West Nile virus, infected mosquitoes transmit a number of other diseases. Here are some of them.

Dengue Fever

Dengue (DENG-gee) fever is a type of virus carried by mosquitoes. Symptoms include high fever, headaches, joint and eye pain, and rashes. Dengue fever can lead to a severe, deadly form of the disease called dengue hemorrhagic fever, which results in blood loss. There is currently no cure for the disease.

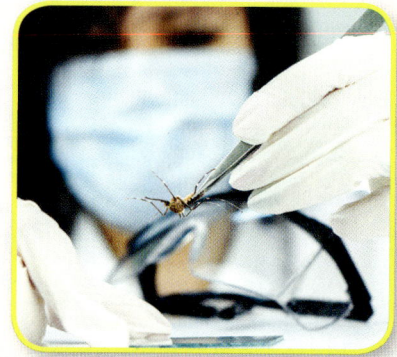

A scientist examines a mosquito

Chikungunya Fever

Chikungunya (chik-un-GUN-yuh) fever is caused by a virus spread by infected mosquitoes. About three to seven days after being bitten, a person has symptoms such as sudden fever, chills, headaches, joint pain, vomiting, and a rash. There is no medicine to prevent Chikungunya. The best treatment is to rest, drink fluids, and take medicine to ease the pain.

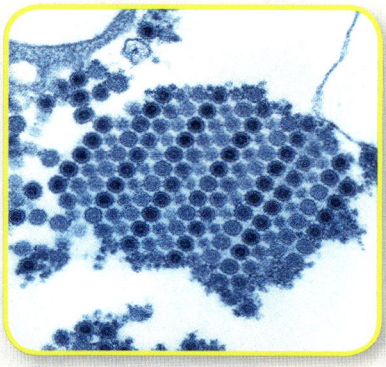

Chikungunya virus particles

Yellow Fever

Yellow fever is a virus commonly found in Africa and South America. The virus lives in a person's body for three to six days until symptoms appear, including fever, **jaundice**, chills, headache, and vomiting. While there is no cure for yellow fever, there is a **vaccine** available to help prevent it.

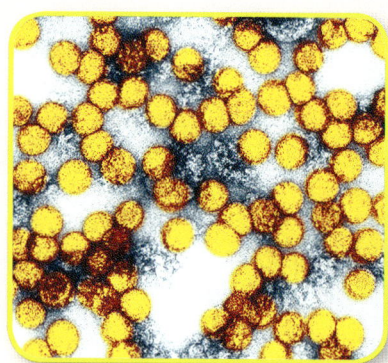

Yellow fever virus particles

Glossary

antennae (an-TEN-ee) the two body parts on an insect's head used for feeling and smelling

borne (BORN) carried by

clotting (KLAHT-ing) becoming thick; when blood clots, it sticks together and stops flowing

cold-blooded (KOHLD-bluhd-id) having a body temperature that changes with the temperature of the surroundings

continent (KON-tuh-nuhnt) one of the world's seven large land masses

defect (DEE-fekt) a fault or weakness in something or someone

drastic (DRAS-tik) extremely severe

encephalitis (en-sef-uh-LYE-tuhss) a swelling of the brain, caused by an infection

hibernate (HYE-bur-nate) to spend the winter in a deep sleep to escape the cold

infected (in-FEK-tid) filled with harmful germs

ingests (in-JESTS) takes into the body through eating or drinking

jaundice (JAWN-dis) the yellowing of the skin and eyes due to illness

kidneys (KID-neez) the pair of body parts that remove waste from the blood and turn water and waste into urine

larva (LAR-vuh) a young insect that has a wormlike body

malaria (muh-LAIR-ee-uh) a deadly disease caused by parasites transmitted by the bite of mosquitoes

mate (MATE) one of a pair of animals that have young together

organs (OR-guhnz) parts of the body that perform particular jobs

parasites (PA-ruh-sites) living things that get food by living on or in another living thing and cause them harm

proboscis (pruh-BOS-uhss) a long, tube-like nose or mouthpart used for feeding

prosthetic (pross-THEH-tik) a device, usually made of steel and plastic, that replaces a missing part of the body

protein (PROH-teen) a kind of substance that keeps the body healthy and strong

pupa (PYOO-puh) the stage in the life cycle of many insects during which the insect changes from a larva to an adult

repellent (rih-PEH-lunt) a chemical that keeps insects and other pests away

saliva (suh-LYE-vah) clear watery liquid found in the mouths of humans and animals

symptoms (SIMP-tuhmz) signs of a disease or other physical problems felt by a person

thrive (THRIVE) to grow or to do well

tissue (TISH-oo) masses of cells that form parts of people and animals

transmit (transs-MIT) to send or pass something from one being to another

vaccine (vak-SEEN) medicine that protects animals and people from a disease

virus (VYE-ruhss) a tiny germ that can be seen only with a powerful microscope; it can invade cells and cause disease

Index

Africa 4–5, 9, 11, 22
Alex the horse 19
body parts, insect 12–13
Brazil 10–11
Chikungunya fever 22
dengue fever 22
eggs 12, 14–15, 16–17
Felipe, Luiz 10–11
habitat 14–15
life stages 16–17
malaria 4–5, 6–7, 8–9, 20–21
parasites 5, 6, 8–9
protection 20–21
repellent, insect 21
size 4–5
West Nile virus 18–19, 21
yellow fever 22
Zika virus 10–11, 21

Bibliography

Keilman, John. "Fight Against Malaria: Battle of Life and Death." *Chicago Tribune* (November 26, 2009).

Spielman, Andrew, and Michael D'Antonio. *Mosquito: The Story of Man's Deadliest Foe.* New York: Hachette (2001).

Centers for Disease Control and Prevention: www.cdc.gov/features/stopmosquitoes/index.html

Read More

Goldish, Meish. *Bloodthirsty Mosquitoes (No Backbone! The World of Invertebrates).* New York: Bearport (2008).

Perish, Patrick. *Mosquitoes (Insects Up Close).* Minnetonka, MN: Bellwether (2018).

Learn More Online

To learn more about mosquitoes, visit
www.bearportpublishing.com/BuggedOut

About the Author

Meish Goldish has written more than 300 books for children. He lives in Brooklyn, New York.